WITHDRAWN

1 0 JUN 2022

*For Charlotte Harrison and Rani Manco,
with thanks to Eleanor Nesbitt – P.M.*

Text copyright © Pratima Mitchell 2002
Illustrations copyright © Alison Bryant 2002
Book copyright © Hodder Wayland 2002

Published in Great Britain in 2002
by Hodder Wayland, an imprint of
Hodder Children's Books.

Consultant: Pritam Singh, an editor of the *International Journal of Punjab Studies*
Editor: Katie Orchard

Cataloguing in Publication Data
Mitchell, Pratima
The Guru's Family: a story about Guru Nanak's Birthday. – (Celebration stories)
1. Sikhism – Juvenile fiction 2. Children's stories
I. Title
823.9'14 [J]

ISBN: 0 7502 3663 9

Printed in Hong Kong by Wing King Tong.

Hodder Children's Books
A division of Hodder Headline Limited
338 Euston Road, London NW1 3BH.

CELEBRATION STORIES

The Guru's Family

PRATIMA MITCHELL

Illustrated by Alison Bryant

HODDER
Wayland

an imprint of Hodder Children's Books

Guru Nanak's Birthday

Celebrating the birthday of the founder of the Sikh religion, and the first Guru, has always been a quiet festival. Exchanging presents, sending cards and spending money isn't how most Sikhs choose to remember Guru Nanak. Instead, they honour him by following his example on a daily basis – they pray to God, work honestly and share the day with others.

Guru Nanak's message was that money does not buy happiness; wealth is nothing to be proud of, and we should share whatever God gives us with our neighbour.

On Guru Nanak's birthday (also known as Gurpurb), Sikhs might wear something new, and give away traditional sweets to friends and relatives. They will certainly go to the Gurdwara (perhaps visit a specially holy or historic Gurdwara) and share a communal meal. Gurpurb is very much a family occasion.

This is a story about two families, separated by distance but united by love, and how they spend Gurpurb in their different ways. They also discover that, thanks to modern technology, they can be connected to one another in a way that would have astonished Guru Nanak, but also pleased him very much!

Staying in Touch

"Baljit, *puttar* – holiday over, eh? So sad
you are all going. Every day we will cry and
remember you."

Simran Aunty held Baljit's cheeks and chin in
one hand and squeezed. Baljit shut his eyes. Her
hand was strong from milking the buffalo and
making *roti*. He couldn't move his face this way
or that.

Grandfather leaned over, resting on his walking stick. "Little bit Panjabi you have learned, little bit our village ways," he said.

Simran Aunty's daughter, Gurprit – Priti for short – grinned. She knew Baljit hated being treated like a baby. She was ten; he was six months younger. They were cousins and also best friends. Of course they were going to miss one another when he went back to England!

Baljit had enjoyed being spoiled by his aunts, uncles, grandparents and cousins. All summer they had given him and his sister, Kamal, presents: clothes, sweets and toys. They had taken them on a pilgrimage to the Golden Temple. Baljit and Kamal had visited Chandigarh, the beautiful modern capital of Panjab. All day they had played in the courtyard. They had eaten sweet mangoes straight off Uncle's trees. They had drunk gallons of delicious fresh buttermilk. Now it was the end of the holiday.

9

The whole family ate their last meal together
under the canopy of the pipal tree in the
courtyard. Through the branches Baljit saw the
stars glittering. How strange that forty-eight
hours later they would be back home in England.

10

He pictured their little house in Coventry. It was hard to imagine wearing shoes and socks again.

"One more story, Simran Aunty," begged Kamal.

Simran Aunty settled comfortably on the string bed and crossed her legs. In her head was a treasure chest of wonderful stories.

"When Guru Nanak was a little boy," she began, "he looked after his father's cattle. He grazed them and made them drink from a pond. It was so hot one day, that he fell asleep in the shade of a big pipal tree, just like ours." She pointed at the tree, then continued.

"A rich man passed by on horseback. He was heading for the forest to hunt. He saw the child Guru in the morning, stretched out under the pipal tree. When he returned in the afternoon, Nanak was still fast asleep. The rich man was amazed. There were no flies on his face, and even though the sun had moved the tree still shaded him. Guru Nanak's face and body were miraculously protected from the sun's glare."

"God was taking care of him," explained Priti to Kamal.

Grandfather said, "Well, may God look after all of you, too. How I wish you could all be here for Gurpurb, Guru Nanak's birthday."

"We will arrange a special reading of the Granth Sahib in the Gurdwara for the whole family," said Simran Aunty. "Our family is scattered over the four corners of the world. Did you know that, Baljit and Kamal? Many years ago our uncles and aunties and cousins went abroad to work."

"In England, in Canada, in Australia *and* in Fiji," Priti added.

"We should make a family website for us all!" laughed Baljit's father.

"Bal and I are going to write e-mails every Tuesday and Thursday," said Priti, hugging her knees. Priti's eighteen-year-old brother, Angad, owned a computer shop in the village. He had just two old computers, but they worked. The local farmers paid Angad to let them use the computers to order seeds and machinery. They kept up with the latest market price for their wheat on the Internet.

"How clever these youngsters are," Simran Aunty said.

"But, Simran, these children can't milk cows or thresh grain, like we did at their age!" said Baljit's mother.

Simran Aunty replied, "They are much smarter than we ever were. This wonderful e-mail will keep us all together as a family. Letters get lost, but e-mail is magic!"

Baljit took a last look at the night sky – it was as if someone had dumped a truckload of diamonds on black velvet. Our family is scattered, he thought, just like those stars.

Angad's Secret

Priti cycled down the lane to Angad's computer shop. She tried counting how many e-mails had been exchanged since Baljit had gone back to England – there were a lot.

Outside the tiny shop was a sign: *Millennium Internet International*. Inside, in front of one computer, sat a very pretty girl.

Angad looked annoyed when Priti came in.
"I've told you not to come here before eight
o'clock," he said between gritted teeth.

Priti smiled sweetly. "I won't tell Mama that
you and Guddi have a date, if that's what you're
worried about."

Guddi turned round quickly, flipping her long
black pigtail. "Please, Priti, it's a secret."

"OK, OK, stop worrying. It's safe with me."
Priti settled herself in front of the second screen
and typed in Baljit's e-mail address…

Hi, Bal,

Sat Sri Akal! Caught Angad and Guddi in the shop.
All alone! G's mum wants her to marry a Sikh boy
in England. But she and Angad are in love...

Got a shock today – that fat lady from the
Gurdwara Committee grabbed me in the lane.
'Big, big honour, Gurprit,' she said. 'You are
chosen to sing in the Kirtan on Guru Nanak's
birthday. Rehearsal is tomorrow at five sharp.
Then three times a week
until November.'

Is she crazy? Remember that frog we used to hear at night when Mama told us stories? Broo, broo. My voice is just like it.

Maddo the buffalo is sick. Her big eyes look so sad, like she's crying. Papaji is in a very bad mood because he has to buy butter and milk from our neighbour. Sorry, have to stop, Angad is shouting that people are waiting to use the computer. I'll e-mail you again on Thursday.

Lots of love to everyone,

Priti

A New Look

When Baljit got back from football practice, his parents were talking in the kitchen. His mother scolded, "Look at you, Baljit. So untidy! You've been dragged backwards through a bush, it seems. Look at your *patka*, look at your hair!"

"Never mind, son," said Dad, laughing. "From this Saturday you'll never have to worry about plaiting your hair, or tying a *patka*, again."

"You mean—" Baljit did a double take. "Fantastic!" He danced around the room as Kamal clapped out a rhythm.

Dear Priti,

You'll never guess! Dad and Mum took me to the barbershop. All my long hair ended up on the floor! Wow. My head feels so light, I keep shaking it to see if it's still there! Now I get up fifteen minutes later. No more combing and plaiting my hair. Mum says it's not practical for Sikh boys in England.

Dad said that a good Sikh is someone who works hard, shares their things and says their prayers. When I'm older I can grow my hair again. Lots of our Canadian cousins did.

What's happening in the village on Gurpurb? How's your singing? What else will you do? Dad has planned a big surprise. Gurpurb is on a Monday. We will go to the Gurdwara in the evening. But Dad says we will do something special on Sunday.

Bye, Bal

Hi, Bal,

Scan us a photo of your new hairstyle!

We had a big drama – Angad and Guddi ran off and got married in the Golden Temple in Amritsar yesterday!!! It feels so grown up to have a sister-in-law! Papaji shouted and got very angry with Angad.

Mama said, 'Just what is the point? No good crying over spilt milk now.' Then she tripped over a stool and the jug she was carrying flew out of her hand. What do you think landed on the floor? A litre of milk, of course! Papaji was even more angry.

Love, Priti

International Greetings

Hi, Priti,

Lots of news. We went to Heathrow. It is
E–N–O–R–M–O–U–S. Much, much bigger than
Amritsar. Hundreds of planes landing, taking off,
taxiing. Rows and rows, parked like cars. I am
definitely going to be an airline pilot when I grow
up. Then I'll come to Amritsar
and pick you up.

We went to meet Toshi Uncle and Sonu Aunty.
It takes them twenty-four hours to fly from
Australia to Canada, and they had to change
planes at Heathrow.

Mum said that Guru Nanak was also a great
traveller, like Columbus. Our class project is on
America, so I know that Christopher Columbus
sailed only a few years before Guru Nanak
was born.

Sonu Aunty had a good idea. She said, 'Choose a greeting card design on the Internet,' (she gave me the web address), 'and send it to every member of our family for Gurpurb.'

Mum said, 'But it's not the custom to send cards. We like to meet everyone and wish them well in the Gurdwara.'

Aunty said, 'Then let's make a new tradition!'

Write a nice message for the card, Priti. You're better than I am at poetry.

Cheers, Bal

Hello, Bal,

What do you think of this:

> *We send you love,*
> *We send you joy,*
> *To all the girls*
> *And all the boys,*

> *Happy Gurpurb! Happy Guru Nanak Day!*

Love, Priti

Dear Priti,

Brill! I will scan a pic of Guru Nanak to go with the message.

Bal

For three days and nights before Gurpurb, the entire Guru Granth Sahib was sung in the village Gurdwara. Everyone slipped off their shoes at the entrance, and sat down inside to think and pray for a while.

Priti and other children sang in the evening services. Her mother worked in the Gurdwara kitchen to make food. A huge pot of *prasad*, made with wheat, butter and sugar, was brought out.

After the service, people who came up to the altar were given a dollop of *prasad*. It was a blessing they could take home.

It was a full moon the night before Gurpurb. Priti and her parents walked home after the evening service. Priti warmed her hands on a lump of delicious hot *prasad*, nibbling as she walked.

Angad and his new bride overtook them in the dusty lane, phut-phutting past on their new scooter – a wedding present from Guddi's parents.

"A story, Mama, please," Priti asked when they got home, snuggling into her quilt.

"Let me just fetch Grandfather his hot milk, and I'll tell you about Bhagat Puran Singh and Piara." But by the time she returned from the kitchen, Priti was fast asleep.

Circling
the Village

In the morning, Grandfather sat under the pipal tree in the courtyard. He was as still as a statue in a grey shawl and bright red turban. Priti heard him saying the morning prayer:

There is one Being
Truth by name
Creator
Without fear
Without hatred
Timeless in form
Self existent
The grace of the Guru.

Guddi put a glass of milky tea into
Grandfather's hand as he ended his prayers.
Then he hobbled to the front door to join
the others, waiting for the procession to pass.

The sound of singing, cymbals and clapping
came nearer.

First came the five Khalsa warriors, dressed in yellow with silver swords hanging from their waists. Behind them came the Guru Granth Sahib, carried all around the village under a canopy of red and yellow silk. The procession circled the village before it was taken into the Gurdwara.

A Special Day

Dear Priti,

I got twenty-three Gurpurb cards on the Internet
– from our cousins in Canada, Melbourne, Fiji and
lots of distant cousins in Glasgow, London,
Solihull, Guyana and California. Our Gurpurb
message worked! Dad is going to try to arrange a
big family get-together next year in the village. I
sent everyone your e-mail address, so you will get
lots of mail, too.

On Sunday we got up at six! It was dark and freezing cold. We drove to Norwich. First Mama drove as far as the Happy Eater. I had orange juice, fried eggs and toast for breakfast. Then Dad drove. We saw a huge statue of Maharajah Dalip Singh in Norwich. He was riding a horse. He was the last king of the Sikhs, but the British soldiers took away his kingdom and gave his MASSIVE diamond, the *Koh-i-Noor*, to Queen Victoria. It's in Queen Elizabeth's crown in the Tower of London.

Afterwards we drove to a huge country house called Elveden Manor. Queen Victoria liked Dalip Singh so much that she gave him this house. He married an Egyptian lady and had five children.

Lots of other Sikh families from all over Britain were at Elveden, because of Gurpurb being the next day. I think they felt homesick. We weren't allowed inside the house, but we walked in the garden. We saw hundreds of tiny plastic *kirpans*. Dad said it was like putting flowers on a grave. Sikh people wanted to remember their last king.

Bye, Bal

Dear Bal,

I am so jealous! I wish I could go to Elveden Manor.

It was nearly like a normal day in the village, except the service was longer. Oh, I forgot – Mama, Guddi and I had new clothes and Grandfather, Papaji and Angad had new turbans. Guddi and Angad were given presents of money from people because they just got married.

After the service someone said to Mama, 'You
must be so proud of your Priti. So sweetly she
sang in the Kirtan, she brought tears to my eyes.'
Don't laugh!

Some of the collection money is sent to a home
for sick people every year. It was started by a very
good man called Puran Singh, who is called the
Mother Theresa of Amritsar.

Love, Priti

PS – I had four e-mails from cousins I've never
even heard of!

Soon after Gurpurb it became too cold to sit in the courtyard after sunset. Storytelling time was at night, on the bed and under Priti's velvet quilt.

Priti's mother said, "Why don't you start sending Kamal and Baljit some of the stories that I tell you? If you're awake this time, I can tell you about Bhagat Puran Singh, who was a true follower of Guru Nanak."

Priti snuggled under the quilt and her mother began. "Puran had nothing of his own, but loved to serve people by helping in the Golden Temple. He swept the floor and nursed the sick. One day on the street he found a very thin, sad looking man called Piara. Piara couldn't walk or talk. He had no home and no one to look after him.

Puran picked Piara up, and carried him around in his arms for the rest of his life. He acted as a human wheelchair. After many years, enough money was collected by Sikhs all over the world to build a home for the homeless in Amritsar, called *Pingalwara*. Everyone in the Panjab has heard of Puran Singh."

Dear Priti,

I printed out the story and read it to Kamal.

Exciting news! Dad is teaching me to make a website. It's going to be our family website. All the cousins have been asked for photos and the story of their lives. Send me a pic of Maddo the buffalo. On the website you can click buttons and go to different pages such as the family photo album, what we are all doing, our village in the Panjab and so on. Isn't it a great idea?

Bye, Baljit

Hi, Bal!

Angad says he will do a newsletter for the family website. Mama says, why not share my bedtime stories with everyone? I tried explaining about e-mail to Grandfather, and about the website. He said he knew that Guru Nanak would one day bring the whole family together! Next year, when lots of the family meet in our village, we won't be strangers to one another. It's like Mama said – e-mail's magic! Keep writing.

Lots of love to you, Kamal, Uncle and Aunty,

Priti

Glossary

Golden Temple The holy Sikh shrine in Amritsar. The temple was built in 1604 by Guru Arjun Dev, the fifth Guru. Sikhs call it *Harmandir Sahib*, 'divine residence of God'.

Gurpurb The birthday of Guru Nanak. *Gur* means 'Guru' and *parab* means 'day of celebration'.

Guru Granth Sahib The Sikh holy book of Scriptures.

Kirpan A small ceremonial dagger worn by Sikhs.

Kirtan A religious service that is sung.

Khalsa A Sikh who has been baptised and follows the religion.

Patka A piece of cloth to keep long hair tidy.

Puttar A Panjabi word, meaning 'son'.

Roti A type of chapatti.

Sat Sri Akal! A Panjabi greeting, meaning 'true and timeless God'.

Salwar kameez Indian dress found mainly in the north. It is made up of a long tunic, loose trousers and a veil worn round the shoulders, known as a *dupatta*.

Thalis Metal trays on which food is served.

46

CELEBRATION STORIES

Look out for these other titles in the **Celebration Stories** series:

Coming Home by Jamila Gavin
It's almost Divali, and there's lots to do. But then Preeta goes missing – and in the world of the gods, a battle rages between good and evil. When the night grows dark, will the Divali candles light everyone safely home?

The Best Prize of All by Saviour Pirotta
Linda has spent months growing a giant pumpkin for the Harvest Festival. She knows she's going to win the prize for the biggest vegetable. But she's not the only one who wants first prize. So when Linda's pumpkin is stolen the night before the competition, she's convinced she knows who's responsible...

The Taste of Winter by Adèle Geras
Naomi is going to talk about Hanukkah at her school's Winter Festivals Assembly. She needs something for the display – but what? Just when she thinks she's found the answer, a perfect solution comes from an unexpected place.

You can buy all these books from your local bookseller, or order them direct from the publisher. For more information about Celebration Stories, write to: *The Sales Department, Hodder Children's Books, a division of Hodder Headline Limited, 338 Euston Road, London NW1 3BH.*